Hello, Family Members,

Learning to read is one of the moents of early childhood. **Hello Reader** help children become skilled readers ning readers learn to read by remen ords like "the," "is," and "and"; by using phonics skills to decode new words; and by interpreting picture and text clues. These books provide both the stories children enjoy and the structure they need to read fluently and independently. Here are suggestions for helping your child *before*, *during*, and *after* reading:

Before
- Look at the cover and pictures and have your child predict what the story is about.
- Read the story to your child.
- Encourage your child to chime in with familiar words and phrases.
- Echo read with your child by reading a line first and having your child read it after you do.

During
- Have your child think about a word he or she does not recognize right away. Provide hints such as "Let's see if we know the sounds" and "Have we read other words like this one?"
- Encourage your child to use phonics skills to sound out new words.
- Provide the word for your child when more assistance is needed so that he or she does not struggle and the experience of reading with you is a positive one.
- Encourage your child to have fun by reading with a lot of expression . . . like an actor!

After
- Have your child keep lists of interesting and favorite words.
- Encourage your child to read the books over and over again. Have him or her read to brothers, sisters, grandparents, and even teddy bears. Repeated readings develop confidence in young readers.
- Talk about the stories. Ask and answer questions. Share ideas about the funniest and most interesting characters and events in the stories.

I do hope that you and your child enjoy this book.

—Francie Alexander
　Reading Specialist,
　Scholastic's Learning Ventures

To the belief that there are two sides to every story
—F.M.

To Bugsy and Chico
—M.S.

Text copyright © 1999 by Faith McNulty.
Illustrations copyright © 1999 by Mavis Smith.
All rights reserved. Published by Scholastic Inc.
SCHOLASTIC, HELLO READER! and CARTWHEEL BOOKS and associated logos are trademarks and/or registered trademarks of Scholastic Inc.

Library of Congress Cataloging-in-Publication Data
McNulty, Faith.
    The silly story of a flea and his dog / by Faith McNulty ;
illustrated by Mavis Smith.
        p. cm. —(Hello reader! Level 3)
    "Cartwheel books."
    Summary: Herman the flea describes the perils that he and his many brothers and sisters face after making their home in the fur of Goldie, a family pet.
ISBN 0-590-22860-9
[1. Fleas—Fiction. 2. Dogs—Fiction.]   I. Smith, Mavis, ill.
II. Title. III. Series.
PZ7.M24Si   1999
[E] — dc21   98-44088
                                                        CIP
                                                        AC

12   11   10   9   8   7   6   5   4   3   2   1   9/9   0/0   01   02   03   04

Printed in the U.S.A.   24
First printing, March 1999

The Silly Story of a Flea and his Dog

by Faith McNulty
Illustrated by Mavis Smith

Hello Reader! — Level 3

SCHOLASTIC INC.
Cartwheel B·O·O·K·S ®
New York   Toronto   London   Auckland   Sydney

Hi there!

I'm a flea named Herman.

Just hold still

while I jump aboard

and tell you the story of my life.

Boy, is it exciting!

One narrow escape after another.

But we fleas are smart—and lucky.

Fleas always win!

I was born in a rug
where my mother laid
a couple of hundred eggs.
I was a tiny little thing,
weak and helpless and hungry.
I ate dust and stuff
and grew quickly.

In a few days I jumped

for the first time.

It was just a little jump,

but I loved it.

I knew I was born to jump.

I jumped again,

so high that I had

a view of the whole world.

I saw an ocean of rug

with flowers on it—

very pretty—

a sofa as big as the Rocky Mountains,

and I saw A DOG!

A lovely, fuzzy, yellow dog,

lying on the rug by the sofa.

It was love at first sight.

I hopped and skipped

across the rug.

My brothers and sisters—

I had lots of them—

hopped beside me.

We were almost there,

when I heard a whistle.

A voice called, "Here, Goldie!"

The dog got up

and ran out of the room.

I sat down and cried.

So did my brothers and sisters.

But we fleas are smart

and we never give up.

We talked it over

and came up with an idea—

go to the place where the dog

had been lying and wait!

So we hopped over.

We could tell by the dog hair

when we got to the right spot.

While we waited, we played games—

tag, hopscotch, hide-and-seek.

I practiced high jumps

and quick turns.

But we were getting hungry.

In fact, I was starving.

I thought, *If that dog doesn't come*

back soon I'll die!

Then I heard footsteps and voices.

Goldie trotted into the room—

and then, *(sob!)* jumped onto the sofa.

Out of reach!

We all wailed.

Then a lady came into the room.

She said, "Goldie!

Get down this minute!

You should be ashamed!"

Goldie jumped off the sofa

and lay down

just where we were waiting.

Singing and laughing,

we jumped aboard.

Life on Goldie

was wonderful.

She didn't seem to notice us.

We ate well. We played games

in the forest of golden hair.

Then she began to scratch.

It was terrifying.

At any moment sharp toenails

might rake through the hair.

I was afraid I'd be crushed

or flung out into space.

I saw that happen to

a couple of my brothers.

But fleas are smart!

I figured out what to do.

At the first scratch,

I hurried down to her paw.

Nestled between her toes,

I rode along safely

while she scratched.

You've got to admit that's clever!

Then the worst happened!

The boy said, "Here, Goldie!"

He got down on the rug

and was petting her,

when Goldie turned on her back.

We weren't ready for this.

The boy saw a few of us
on her tummy, running for shelter.
He yelled, "Mom! Goldie has fleas!"
"I thought so," said Mom.
"Give her a bath."

The next thing I know,
we're all in the tub.
Water is raining down.
We're getting soaked.
Goldie is shivering
and scrambling.

The boy is holding her collar
and saying, "Be good! Keep still!"
I am terrified.
My whole world is shivering
and shaking and wet!
I see brothers and sisters
swept away — down the drain!

I run up to Goldie's neck,

where the hair is thick,

and hang on.

I'm safe for a moment.

GOLDIE

Then soapsuds wash over me

in waves of foam.

I let go. I'm swept down.

I don't know where I am.

There is soap in my eyes and mouth.

"Keep still while I rinse you,"

the boy says.

Clear water washes over me.

I lose my grip.

I'm washed along by a river
that splashes down into the tub.
I can see the hole where
the water gurgles down.
I see brothers and sisters disappear!

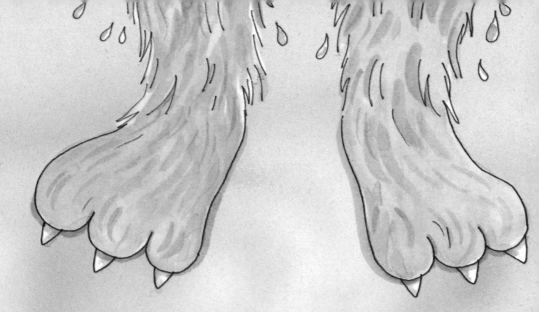

I'm in the water, whirling around.

I think I'm doomed,

but then I see Goldie's paw.

If only I can reach it!

Kicking against the current,
I make it. I seize a tuft of hair,
climb aboard, and hold on tight.

A moment later, Goldie is

out of the tub,

being dried with a towel.

I lie low, hidden between her toes.

When the danger has passed,
I climb her leg.
I run through nice, clean fur
up to her back. I find a few of
my brothers and sisters there.
We all agree it is great to be alive.

The life of a flea is dangerous.

But we are smart. We are lucky.

At least a few of us always win!